Angelina and the Rag Doll

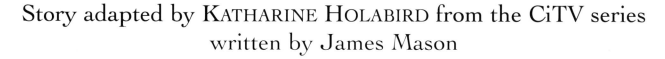

Story adapted by KATHARINE HOLABIRD from the CiTV series
written by James Mason

BASED ON THE CLASSIC PICTURE BOOKS
BY KATHARINE HOLABIRD AND HELEN CRAIG

PUFFIN BOOKS

PUFFIN BOOKS

Published by the Penguin Group
Penguin Books Ltd, 80 Strand, London WC2R 0RL, England
Penguin Putnam Inc., 375 Hudson Street, New York, New York 10014, USA
Penguin Books Australia Ltd, 250 Camberwell Road, Camberwell, Victoria 3124, Australia
Penguin Books Canada Ltd, 10 Alcorn Avenue, Toronto, Ontario, Canada M4V 3B2
Penguin Books India (P) Ltd, 11 Community Centre, Panchsheel Park, New Delhi – 110 017, India
Penguin Books (NZ) Ltd, Cnr Rosedale and Airborne Roads, Albany, Auckland, New Zealand
Penguin Books (South Africa) (Pty) Ltd, 24 Sturdee Avenue, Rosebank 2196, South Africa

Penguin Books Ltd, Registered Offices: 80 Strand, London WC2R 0RL, England

www.penguin.com

First published 2002
5 7 9 10 8 6 4

British Library Cataloguing in Publication Data
A CIP catalogue record for this book is available from the British Library

ISBN 0-140-56890-5

To find out more about Angelina, visit her web site at
www.angelinaballerina.com

Angelina couldn't wait to tell her best friend, Alice, the exciting news.

"Miss Lilly needs a helper for the beginner's ballet class," Angelina announced proudly as they walked home together, "and she asked ME!"

The two little mouselings went to Mrs Thimble's General Store to buy some sweets to celebrate.

"Don't forget my second-hand box," Mrs Thimble reminded them as they were about to leave. "Just bring anything you don't need any more and it will help a good cause."

When she got home, Angelina made a collection of all the things she'd outgrown.

"What's this?" asked Alice, holding up an old rag doll mouse in a torn tutu.

"Oh, that's Polka," said Angelina. "We used to dance together when I first started at Miss Lilly's Ballet School."

"Where did you get her?" Alice asked.

"I don't remember," said Angelina. "But I'm too grown-up for her now."

Angelina added Polka to the collection, and the next morning the two mouselings carried all Angelina's old clothes and toys to the General Store, and everything went straight into Mrs Thimble's second-hand box.

The following week, Angelina's Grandpa and Grandma came for tea and decided to have a look at Angelina's baby photographs.

"Ahh," said Grandma, smiling. "Here's a picture of you at your first ballet lesson, with Polka."

"Do you remember the day I won Polka for you at the fair?" Grandpa asked. "And you said you'd never ever let her go."

"Y-y-yes, Grandpa," Angelina stammered, suddenly remembering.

"You called her Polka because that was the special dance we always did together," Grandpa said. "Let's see if we can still remember it." But Angelina was already running out the door. "I'm sorry," Angelina called, "but I forgot to tell Alice something important!"

Angelina ran all the way
to Alice's cottage to tell
her the terrible news.
"We've got to get Polka back!"
Angelina shouted. They raced
off together as fast as they
could to Mrs Thimble's
General Store.
The two mouselings searched in
all Mrs Thimble's second-hand
boxes, but Polka was nowhere
to be found.
"I'm afraid your doll's already
been taken," Mrs Thimble said.

Angelina couldn't believe that Polka was gone.
She made big posters with Polka's picture on them
and stuck them all around the village. But nobody brought
Polka back.
Then Angelina went up and down the streets with Alice,
and asked about Polka at every shop and doorfront, but
everyone just shook their heads.

Finally, Angelina and Alice went to see Miss Twitchett, who collected things for charity.

"I've just sent all the toys to the poor children in Dacovia," Miss Twitchett said.

"What am I going to do?" Angelina cried.

"At least you'll have fun helping Miss Lilly at ballet school tomorrow," Alice kindly reminded her.

Angelina couldn't let Miss Lilly down, so the next morning she put on her tutu and went to help with the ballet lessons.

All the little dancers were happily crowding around Miss Lilly, but one small mouseling was too shy to join in.

"Come in and sit down, Mary," said Miss Lilly, smiling.
But Mary shook her head and stayed by herself in the corner, clutching an old rag doll.

Angelina looked closer – and gasped. She couldn't believe her eyes – little Mary was holding Polka!

"Excuse me, she's my . . ." Angelina stopped herself. She could see that Mary really loved Polka. "She's a lovely doll," Angelina said with a smile. "And she loves to dance. May I show you?" Mary nodded and handed Polka to Angelina.

Angelina began to dance with Polka, the way she always used to, and little Mary smiled and forgot about feeling so shy. Soon she was laughing and dancing around and around the room with Angelina and Polka.

"Well done, darlings." Miss Lilly clapped her hands.

For the rest of the lesson, Mary followed Angelina, and tried to do all the ballet exercises just the way Angelina showed her.

At the end of the morning, Angelina waited with Miss Lilly to say goodbye to all the new ballet students.

"See you next week, Mary," said Angelina.

"I hope I can be a beautiful dancer like you some day," said Mary smiling.

"I'm sure you will," Angelina encouraged her.

Mary hugged Polka. "I'm going to call her Angelina. Is that all right?"

"Yes," said Angelina quietly. "I'd really like that."

The next time that Grandma and Grandpa came to tea, Angelina told them all about Polka and Mary. "I loved Polka and I'm really sorry for breaking my promise to you, Grandpa," Angelina said.

"You did a very grown-up thing," said Grandpa. "I'm really proud of you, Angelina."

Angelina gave her Grandpa an enormous hug, and Mr Mouseling started to play his violin.

"May I have the honour of this dance?" asked Grandpa with a bow.

Angelina curtsied. Then she and Grandpa laughed and danced around the cottage while her father played the polka, and Angelina was absolutely delighted because she still remembered every step!